MW01474350

Helping You Through A Loss

HOW TO HELP SHARE YOUR FEELINGS

CINDY MOYNES

authorHOUSE

AuthorHouse™
1663 Liberty Drive
Bloomington, IN 47403
www.authorhouse.com
Phone: 833-262-8899

© 2021 Cindy Moynes. All rights reserved.

No part of this book may be reproduced, stored in a retrieval system, or transmitted by any means without the written permission of the author.

Published by AuthorHouse 07/20/2021

ISBN: 978-1-6655-3248-8 (sc)
ISBN: 978-1-6655-3247-1 (e)

Print information available on the last page.

Any people depicted in stock imagery provided by Getty Images are models, and such images are being used for illustrative purposes only. Certain stock imagery © Getty Images.

Presented by Cindy Moynes
Illustrated by Cindy Moynes

This book is printed on acid-free paper.

Because of the dynamic nature of the Internet, any web addresses or links contained in this book may have changed since publication and may no longer be valid. The views expressed in this work are solely those of the author and do not necessarily reflect the views of the publisher, and the publisher hereby disclaims any responsibility for them.

This is for Children
Aged 7 – 12
Who've lost a Grandparent

Can you draw how you're feeling today?

People die because of different reasons.

They may be old, they may be really sick, or maybe they died in an accident.

No matter how they died, it wasn't your fault because of something you said or didn't do.

Can your draw or write about something you love to do with someone special?

When someone you love dies,
it just means that the body
has stopped working.

Their heart has stopped beating,
and they don't need food or water.

This could happen to your
Grandma or Grandpa.

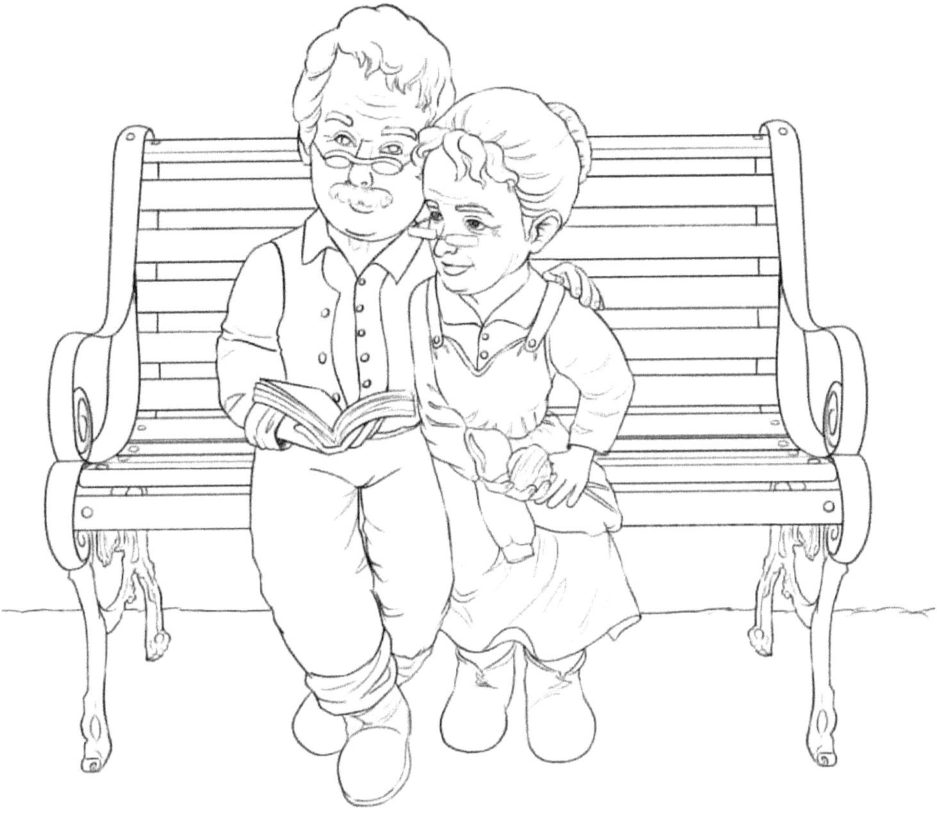

Saying goodbye to your Grandma or Grandpa can be very difficult.

You may have so many different feelings that you may not understand.

You could be sad and angry, and it may be hard to tell them apart.

Can you write about how it makes you feel when you say good bye to someone?

Mom and Dad may be upset.

They may show it by
crying, and/or anger.

Don't worry, they are
NOT angry with you.

Hug them a lot, and ask questions
about Grandma or Grandpa.

This will help them and you
with any sad feelings.

After your Grandma or Grandpa have died, there may be a funeral ceremony.

This is when family members, and friends who knew them, get together and talk about how much they will be missed and most importantly how much they were loved. People may bring flowers, pictures, or food.

This is a great time to say good-bye to that person.

When you are at the funeral, you may see an urn, this is where their ashes will be kept, or you may see Grandma or Grandpa in a casket.

It's alright to touch their hand, and to talk to them.

It's okay to tell them how much you're going to miss them and how much you love them.

Have you ever seen a cemetery?

This maybe where your loved one will be buried after they die.

This is not a scary place, but rather a quiet, peaceful area.

This is where you can visit, place flowers, just sit and talk to your Grandma or Grandpa.

You do not need to be at the cemetery to talk with your Grandma or Grandpa.

Even though you cannot physically see them, their spirit is always close by.

You will always carry them with you in your heart.

They can hear YOU no matter where you are.

You might feel sad, and want to cry.

You miss them, and that's okay.

This is a part of grieving, it's normal, and it's okay to tell someone when you feel sad and upset.

Talking about your feelings, may help you understand why you feel this way. It may help you feel better when you talk.

Sharing your emotions is a great way to express yourself.

Maybe drawing a picture of how you feel, then showing it to someone you trust, so they can sit with you and talk about it.

Maybe just draw a feeling face to show how sad, upset, or how angry you are.

This is a great way for you to share your feelings.

What kind of picture would you draw here?

Maybe making a memory box is something you would enjoy.

Your mom/dad/sister/ or a friend could help you gather up some of your special memories to put into it.

Like a favorite picture, a special book, a blanket, or maybe some favorite jewelry of theirs that you liked.

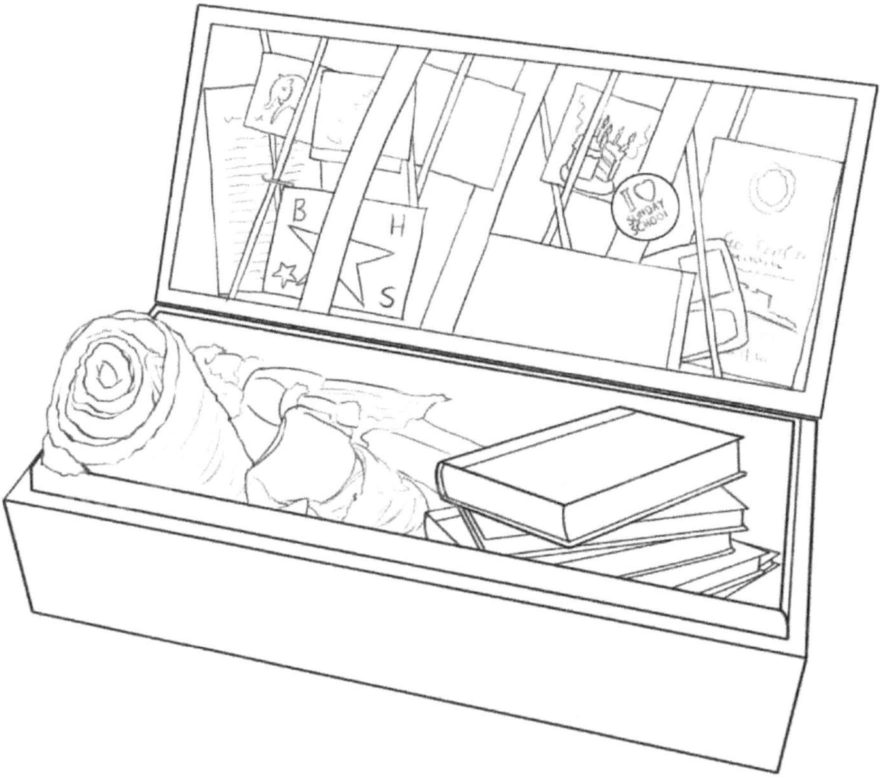
B
H
S
I ♥
SUNDAY
SCHOOL

What would you put in your memory box?

Nobody knows what happens after the person dies, but it's important to ask other people what they think happens.

Different cultures and religions have different beliefs, be sure to ask mom or dad what they think happens.

It helps to talk and ask questions for you to understand.

What kind of picture would you draw here?

No matter what you're feeling,
remember, it's important for
you to talk to someone.

There is no right or wrong way
because they are your feelings.

Don't be ashamed of how you feel,
and don't be afraid to ask for a hug.

You will always have a special
place in your heart for them.

Try not to be upset with your
friends if they do not really
talk to you about the death.

They are sad for you, and just
don't know what to say, or how
to make you feel better.

It's okay if you start the conversation
about how you feel or how much you
miss your Grandma or Grandpa.

Remember you are not alone,
and talking will help.

Most importantly, is to remember, that Grandma and Grandpa always loved you.

They are never truly gone.

They will always be in your heart and in the memories that you shared together.

Think about a special time you shared;

Can you write about a favorite day?

A special date:

Where you were:

What you did:

Who was with you:

Can you draw your favorite time you spent with Grandma, Grandpa or your family?

CPSIA information can be obtained
at www.ICGtesting.com
Printed in the USA
BVHW030337260821
614918BV00001B/67